ALICE in WONDERLAND

Modern Publishing
A Division of Unisystems, Inc./New York, New York 10022

One summer day, Alice and her sister were reading in the meadow. Suddenly a White Rabbit wearing a coat and hat ran past. He pulled out a pocket watch and exclaimed, ''Oh dear! I'm late!''

''How curious!'' said Alice, and she ran after him.

Alice followed the Rabbit down a rabbit hole.
Along the sides of the rabbit hole were amazing
things—maps, mirrors, teapots, and fruit.

"How *very* curious!" Alice exclaimed. Finally
she landed—PLOP!—in a soft bed of leaves.

Alice watched the Rabbit run through a tiny door in a hallway. ''Oh dear! I'm too big to get through the door!'' she thought, bursting into tears. Alice cried and cried until the floor was wet with tears.

Then Alice noticed a bottle that said "DRINK ME!" And without a second thought, she did! Suddenly she began shrinking! Soon she was just the right size to fit through the tiny door.

Alice stepped through the door, and SPLASH!—she was up to her chin in saltwater. It was a pool of tears she had cried when she was so tall! "Oh dear! I don't want to drown in my own tears!" she said.

"Swim this way to shore," said a friendly Dodo bird.

Just as she dried off, the White Rabbit ran by again saying, "Oh my ears and whiskers, how late it's getting! The Queen will have my head." Then he spotted Alice. "Quick! Run home and get my gloves and fan," he told her.

The Rabbit's house was not far away. Alice
quickly found the fan and gloves—and another
little bottle. "Something interesting is bound to
happen if I drink this," she said. So she did!
BOOM! Her head hit the ceiling!

"Kill the giant!" the White Rabbit shouted. His friends began throwing rocks at Alice. Luckily, the rocks turned into tea cakes when they hit her.

"I may as well eat these," Alice thought. As soon as she swallowed one, she began to grow smaller.

Finally Alice was small enough
to escape from the Rabbit's house.
Wandering in the woods, she came
upon a large mushroom. Sitting on
it was a caterpillar. "Who are you?"
he asked.

"I've been so many sizes today,
I don't know *who* I am!" said Alice.
"But I don't think I'm *my* size yet."

"Well then, I have just one
thing to say," said the Caterpillar.
"One side makes you taller; the
other side makes you shorter."

"One side of what?" asked Alice.

"Why, the mushroom," he said.

Alice broke off a piece from each side of the mushroom. She nibbled on one side of it, then the other. First she shrank, then she grew. Her neck stretched out like a giraffe's and she banged her head against a bird's nest. "A serpent!" the bird shrieked. "Get away from my eggs!"

"Oh dear," said Alice. So she nibbled more mushroom—first one side, then the other. Finally she was just her right size. "Now what will happen?" she wondered.

"Where are you going?" said a voice. Alice turned around to see a Cheshire cat sitting in a tree.

"I don't care where I go as long as I get *somewhere*," said Alice.

"Then it doesn't matter which way you go," said the Cat. "The Hatter lives this way. And the March Hare lives that way."

At that, the Cheshire Cat began to disappear—first his tail and then his back paws. Finally all that was left was his grin. Then, that was gone, too.

"Things just get curiouser and curiouser," said Alice as she headed to the Hatter's house.

The Hatter was having tea on the lawn with the March Hare and a sleeping dormouse. When he saw Alice he shouted, "No room!"

"Why, there's plenty of room," said Alice, sitting down.

"Have some tea," said the March Hare.

Just as Alice had filled her teacup and put a cake on her plate, the Hatter shouted out, "Change places!" Everyone got up and moved down a chair. Poor Alice found herself sitting in front of an empty cup and plate.

Just then she saw a door in a tree. "Everything is so curious today, I may as well go in," she thought. And so she did.

Inside the door was a garden. Two gardeners were busy painting white roses with red paint.

"Why are you painting the roses?" asked Alice.

"We were supposed to plant a red rose bush," said one gardener. "If the Queen finds out it's . . ."

"OFF WITH THEIR HEADS!" It was the Queen.

"Never mind!" said the Queen. "Time for court!"

The Jack of Hearts was on trial for stealing the Queen's tarts.

"Off with his head," the Queen shouted.

"Not yet!" said the King. "We have to hear the witnesses."

The first witness was the Hatter. He was told to take off his hat. "I can't," he said. "It isn't mine."

"Then take off his head!" screamed the Queen.

"This is a very curious trial," thought Alice. "Oh dear, now I'm beginning to feel very curious!"

"Stop crowding me," the Dormouse said to Alice.

"I can't help it," Alice replied. "I'm growing."

"Anyone taller than a mile must leave the court," declared the King. Everyone stared at Alice. She tried to stand up and knocked over the jury box.

"Off with her head!" the Queen commanded
her guards who surrounded Alice.

"I'm not afraid of you," Alice declared.
"You're just a deck of cards!" At that all the cards
rose into the air and flew around her. Alice
screamed and suddenly found herself in the
meadow again.

"Wake up, Alice," her sister said. "You've had
quite a nap."

"I had the most curious dream!" Alice
exclaimed. And she told her sister all about
her adventures.

24